THERE WAS AN OLD LADY WHO SWALLOWED FLY GUY

Tedd Arnold

Cartwheel
·B·O·O·K·S·®

SCHOLASTIC INC.
New York   Toronto   London   Auckland
Sydney   Mexico City   New Delhi   Hong Kong

For Marissa, Benjamin, Ethan,
Gary, and Amy — of course!
—T. A.

Copyright © 2007 by Tedd Arnold. Published by Scholastic Inc.

Library of Congress Cataloging-in-Publication Data

Arnold, Tedd.
There was an old lady who swallowed Fly Guy/ Tedd Arnold.
p. cm.
"Cartwheel books."
Summary: After accidentally swallowing her grandson's pet fly, Grandma
tries to retrieve it by consuming progressively larger animals.
ISBN 978-0-439-63906-4
[1. Flies--Fiction. 2. Pets--Fiction. 3. Grandmothers--Fiction. 4.
Humorous stories.] I. Title.

PZ7 .A7379TH 2007   [E]--DC22

2006037714

ISBN 978-0-439-63906-4

21 20 19 18 17 16 15 14 13   13 14

Printed in China 38
First printing, September 2007

A young boy named Buzz
had a pet fly.
No one knows why
he had a pet fly.
Buzz named him Fly Guy.

<u>Chapter 1</u>

One day Buzz went
to visit his grandma.
Fly Guy went, too.

Grandma was happy
to see Buzz.
She ran to hug him.

"Hi, Grandma!" said Buzz.
"I want you to meet my pet..."

Grandma said—

and she swallowed Fly Guy.

Buzz didn't know why
she swallowed Fly Guy.

Chapter 2

Fly Guy went down
a deep dark hole.

At the bottom of the hole,
he came to a wet place.

He looked around for a while.
Then he wanted to leave.

He started up the hole.

Just then, Grandma
swallowed a spider
to catch Fly Guy.

She swallowed a bird
to catch the spider.

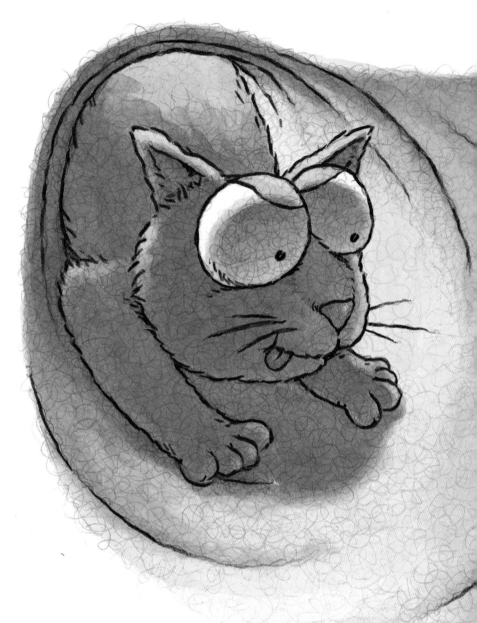

She swallowed a cat
to catch the bird.

She swallowed a dog
to catch the cat.

She swallowed a goat
to catch the dog.

She swallowed a cow
to catch the goat.

Chapter 3

Grandma was about to swallow a horse
to catch the cow.

Fly Guy cried, BUZZ!

"I'm up here!" yelled Buzz.

Out came Fly Guy.

Out came the spider,
the bird, the cat, the dog,
the goat, and the cow.

And everyone lived
happily ever after,
of course!